Shaun O'Day of Ireland

SHAUN O'DAY OF IRELAND

SHAUN O'DAY
of IRELAND

BY

MADELINE BRANDEIS

Producer of the Motion Pictures

"The Little Indian Weaver"
"The Wee Scotch Piper"
"The Little Dutch Tulip Girl"
"The Little Swiss Wood Carver"

Distributed by Pathé Exchange, Inc., New York City

Photographic Illustrations made in Ireland by the Author

 This book, while produced under wartime conditions, in full compliance with government regulations for the conservation of paper and other essential materials, is **COMPLETE AND UNABRIDGED**

GROSSET & DUNLAP
PUBLISHERS   NEW YORK
by arrangement with the A. Flanagan Company

PRINTED IN THE UNITED STATES OF AMERICA

PREFACE

When I began to write these stories about children of all lands I had just returned from Europe whither I journeyed with Marie and Ref. Maybe you don't know Marie and Ref. I'll introduce them: Please meet Marie, my very little daughter, and Ref, my very big reflex camera.

These two are my helpers. Marie helps by being a little girl who knows what other little girls like and by telling me; and Ref helps by snapping pictures of everything interesting that Marie and I see on our travels. I couldn't get along without them.

Several years have gone by since we started our work together and Marie is a bigger girl—but Ref hasn't changed one bit. Ref hasn't changed any more than my interest in writing these books for you. And I hope that *you* hope that I'll never change, because I want to keep on writing until we'll have no more countries to write about—unless, of course, some one discovers a new country.

Even if a new country isn't discovered, we'll find foreign children to talk about—maybe the children in Mars! Who knows? Nobody. Not even Marie—and Marie usually knows about most things. That's the reason why, you see, though I sign myself

Madeline Brandeis

I am really only

Marie's Mother.

DEDICATION

To every child of every land,
  Little sister, little brother,
As in this book your lives unfold,
  May you learn to love each other.

CONTENTS

PART I

PART II

WILL YOU WALK INTO MY STORY—?

Just because I think it may interest you to know it:—In these photographs Kit Wain posed for Shaun O'Day. Kit is a real Irish boy, but he did not have the adventures that Shaun had in the story. He has had many other adventures, however, because Kit is a young actor. Dawn O'Day was played by Mary Jo Desmond. Mary Jo is just a little schoolgirl like you. She looked so much like Dawn O'Day in the story that I asked her to be Dawn for me. And because she is Irish and loves make-believe, she did it.

When Shaun grew older it was Maurice Murphy who posed. Maurice has had a wonderful life for a young boy. He has played on the stage and in motion pictures and also on the piano! For he is a very talented young musician. Maybe you remember seeing him act in the film called "Beau Geste."

Little saucy Marjorie was posed by a little saucy miss who is known as Carmencita Johnson. I should say "well known" because Carmencita, though only five, is already a picture star. She is a very interesting young person, and if I began to tell you all about her and her family of sisters and brothers it would take up all the book and leave no room for the story.

John O'Day, Shaun's son, is portrayed by another little film artist. His name is Gordon Thorpe. Gordon is only six. But he has appeared in more than sixty motion pictures. Do you remember the little Prince in Douglas Fairbanks' "The Iron Mask?" That was Gordon. And in "The Bridge of San Luis Rey"? You surely recognized him.

WILL YOU WALK INTO MY STORY — ?

Dick Good was the fighting boy who didn't believe that Marjorie was a fairy. And of course I need not tell you that the scenes of cities and buildings and places in Ireland were all played by those cities and buildings and places *themselves*.

That is, when I was in Ireland I asked them to pose for me. And they did it willingly the way the children did. They posed very well, in fact. Very quietly.

Only the rain in Ireland is not willing. The rain does not want photographers to catch the beauty of the country. The rain tries to spoil everything for the poor photographers. But we forgive him because he makes Ireland so green.

Here are the names of the little children who helped me so nicely by coming to Marjorie's birthday party and posing as her guests: Alice and Howard Bucquet, Caroline Kuhns, Barbara and Patrick Ford, Betty and Stephen Kline, Marie Madeleine Brandeis and Dietrich Haupt.

The only grown-up in the story, John's girl-fairy, is Miss Alice White. Miss White is such a busy star that I think I should thank her for stopping long enough from her work to be John's girl-fairy in the pages of this book. And I think I should thank all the rest of these good people, even if they are only little people, for they too, are busy. And it is sometimes hard to tear oneself away from the work of the world and walk into a fairy tale.

But these in the photographs did it. And that is what I am going to ask you, young readers, to do now. Come along! See if you can!

MADELINE BRANDEIS.

UPPER LAKE KILLARNEY

Shaun O'Day of Ireland

PART I

CHAPTER I

ISN'T IT A GREAT WONDER?

> The wee word "why"
> Is a fairy gift
> To little babes at birth,
> It opens wide the wonder world
> To every child on earth.

Isn't it a great wonder—the fair green Emerald Isle?

And do you know why Ireland is so green? It is because the rain fairies love Ireland. They have made it the greenest spot on earth. They do be sprinkling it forever with the drops of their fairy rain.

WEE HOUSES COVERED WITH STRAW ROOFS

Ireland is divided into four provinces. They are Ulster, Leinster, Munster, and Connaught.

In Connaught is the County of Galway. In the County of Galway is the District of Connemara.

In Connemara there is a village that

looks out upon a lake. And in that village are wee houses covered with thatched roofs—roofs of straw.

Inside one of these houses there lived a boy, Shaun O'Day. But I am not going to tell you now about Shaun O'Day, nor of the strange thing that befell him. Not now.

First, I shall tell you about his country. I shall tell you about his country because all children love to know the why and the wonder of things. And great is the wonder of Ireland.

This is the tale of the Province of Connaught and how it got its name. Long ago the western districts of Ireland were named after the person who took possession of them.

At this time there reigned a powerful king whose name was Conn. He
was good as well as great, and dearly
loved by his people.

His Queen was equally beloved. Her
name was Eda. Their son was a blessed
and good boy. They named him Conn-
eda, after both his parents.

As Conn-eda grew to manhood, his
strength and goodness grew with his
years. All was harmony in the west
until a great sorrow fell upon the land.
The Queen died. The country mourned
for a year and a day.

And then the King married again.
But the new Queen was not good and
kind as Queen Eda had been. She was
wicked and cruel.

CONNEMARA PEOPLE ENGAGED IN SPINNING

She had several children of her own, and was jealous of Conn-eda, who was the favorite of the King and the darling of the people.

She clearly foresaw that Conn-eda would be King after the death of his father. She wanted her own son to become King some day.

And so she planned to destroy Conn-eda or have him exiled from the country. With envy and hatred in her heart, the wicked Queen went to consult a witch.

The witch gave the Queen a chessboard and told her to invite Prince Conn-eda to play a game of chess.

The witch said to the Queen, "The loser of this game shall be obliged to obey the orders of the winner. And, you, great Queen, shall win the game! Having won the game, you are to send the Prince Conn-eda upon a dangerous journey. He must seek and bring to you, within a year and a day, three golden apples, a magical black steed, and the Hound of Supernatural Powers. These things are so well guarded that the Prince will surely lose his life in attempting to seek them."

The Queen was delighted and hastened to invite Conn-eda to play a game of chess. He agreed to the conditions of the game, and it came about as the witch had promised. The wicked Queen won.

But so pleased was she with her tri-

SUBSTANTIAL HOMES IN A WOODLAND SETTING ON THE KILLARNEY RIVER

umph and so greedy for further power that she challenged the Prince to another game. To the Queen's astonishment and horror, Conn-eda won this second game.

"Since you won the first game," said Conn-eda, "you shall be first to command your reward."

The Queen said, "My reward shall be the three golden apples, the Black Steed, and the Hound of Supernatural Powers. These you must seek and bring to me within the space of a year and a day. If you fail you must leave your country forever or lose your life."

Conn-eda answered, "Then my order to you is that you sit upon the topmost spire of yonder tower until I return.

If I do not return, you may come down at the end of the year and a day."

Conn-eda was troubled and went to consult with a great Druid. The poor Prince had no idea how he was to find these magical treasures.

The great Druid gave the Prince a little, shaggy pony. He bade Conn-eda obey this little horse.

After further instructions from the great Druid, Conn-eda mounted the shaggy steed and set out upon his journey.

His adventures were many. Through them all, the little shaggy horse helped and guided him. The animal had the power of speech.

After days of hardship and danger,

Conn-eda reached the walls of a great city. Two huge towers stood on either side of the gate and sent forth flames of fire. The pony bade Conn-eda alight from his back and take from his ear a small knife.

"With this knife," said the steed, "kill me! Then wrap yourself in my skin, and you shall be able to pass the gates of the city unharmed. All I ask is that you return to my body and pour a drop of this powerful ointment upon my poor flesh."

With these words the pony gave Conn-eda a bottle of magic fluid.

The Prince cried, "Never, never! I would rather die than kill you, my good friend!"

But at last the pony persuaded Conneda, and the Prince stabbed his noble steed. His heart bled, and he was in despair at what he had done.

But he suddenly thought of the bottle of fluid which the steed had given him. Following the animal's advice, the Prince poured the ointment over the horse's body.

No sooner had he done this than the horse's shape changed to the form of a handsome young man.

"Behold!" cried the noble youth. "You have freed me from a wicked enchantment. I am brother of the King of the city. It was a wicked Druid who kept me so long in the form of a shaggy steed. Now, through your brave

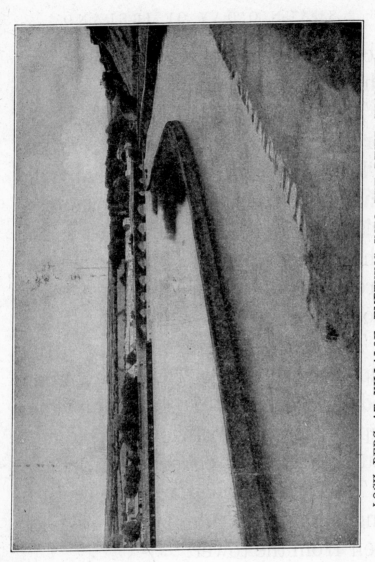

LOCH DERG AT KILLALOE, EMPTYING INTO THE RIVER SHANNON

act, you have broken the spell, and I shall help you in your quest."

The handsome Prince asked his brother, the King, for those treasures which Conn-eda sought. Gladly did the King give to him the apples from his magic tree, the Black Steed, and the precious hound. With these three treasures did Conn-eda return to his country.

The wicked Queen, who was sitting upon the top of her tower, saw Conn-eda approaching. She saw him riding upon a prancing steed and leading a curious animal by a silver chain.

The Queen knew that he was returning in triumph. In despair she cast herself from the tower.

That was her end. And that was also the end of trouble in the kingdom of the west. For at the death of the good King Conn, his son Conn-eda was made king. Conn-eda ruled wisely, and it was after his name that the province of Connaught was called.

In Connaught is the County of Galway. Sheep are raised in Galway. And it has a rugged, wild seacoast.

It was on this coast that the wreck of part of the Spanish Armada took place in 1588. For this reason there is still to be found, in this part of Ireland, people of Spanish descent. And the fairies are said to love the County of Galway. In Galway County is the District of Connemara.

Once upon a time there dwelt a powerful family named Conmac. In Irish "Connemara" means "Seaside of the Conmacs," for it was this wild and rocky shore that was used by these ancient royal people as their seaside.

Connemara is called the Congested District of Ireland. The word "congested" means "overcrowded." But in this case it does not mean that the country is overcrowded with people. For the people are few here in this wild land.

But the barren soil does not yield enough for those few people. And there is much poverty in Connemara.

But there also are lakes of great beauty, and valuable marble, known

IRISH FARMER AND HIS SON PATCHING THE ROOF OF
THEIR OLD STONE HOUSE

as Connemara marble. And there are fairies! Well do the fairies love Connemara!

In Connemara there is a village, and in that village lived a boy named Shaun O'Day.

Do you know the why of that name Shaun? It is the same as the name John. But it is an Irish name. It is spelled "Sean" in Irish and pronounced "hwan."

It is Jean in French, and Giovanni in Italian, and Hans in German, and Ivan in Russian. It is Juan in Spanish, Jock in Scotch, and Johnny in American.

It is a Hebrew word and has a very beautiful meaning: "Gift of God." Do you wonder that so many boys all over the world are given the name John?

Here we have the why and the wonder of the land of Shaun O'Day. So now we shall hear of the strange things that befell this lad, who lived in the Emerald Isle.

CHAPTER II

SHAUNEEN AND THE LEPRECHAUN

"Can you not catch the tiny clamor,
  Busy click of an elfin hammer,
  Voice of the Leprechaun ringing shrill
  As he busily plies his trade?"
                              —W. B. YEATS

We have been speaking of the fairies and how they love Ireland.

The fairies are divided into tribes just the way Ireland itself is divided into many districts, counties, and provinces.

There are many tribes of fairies, and these tribes are all quite different from one another.

There are those who dress like the

flowers; and those that change themselves into various shapes. There are evil fairies and solitary fairies.

You must always call them the "Good People," for they are easily offended.

But if you believe in them and leave a bit of milk for them upon the window sill, they will bring luck and happiness to you.

Now the fairy that we are going to meet in this story is called the leprechaun, or fairy shoemaker. We are going to meet him, because if it had not been for him, there would be no story at all.

The fairy shoemaker sits under a toadstool making tiny shoes. The word "leprechaun" comes from two Irish words meaning "one shoe." The reason he bears this name is because he is always working upon one shoe.

The leprechaun is quick and mysterious. He is also mischievous. And one of his great pranks is stealing wee boys away.

He steals wee Irish boys away from their homes because they do work so well. He makes them work for himself—this mischief-making fairy!

He will not bother with wee girls.

"Wee girls are not so strong as wee boys," says he.

So when you meet Shaun O'Day, you must not be surprised to find him wearing a petticoat! You must not be

HE WORE A FLANNEL PETTICOAT

surprised, because it is the fault of the leprechaun.

You see, Shaun O'Day lived in a very western part of Ireland, in Connemara, where fairies abound.

And in the village where he lived, the boys were all dressed in red petticoats! They were dressed in red flannel petticoats until they reached a tall and manly age.

This was many years ago. And though they would not tell you why they wore those petticoats, I am telling you 'twas because of the leprechauns.

Every wee boy's mother feared the leprechaun. And so she dressed her boy in the dress of the girl to trick that sly creature.

Boys were needed badly by the human folk. Why should the fairy folk be taking them away?

Shaun had a good, kind father. He was a fisherman. Shaun's mother was dead.

But Shaun and his father lived happily enough until one day Shaun's father married again.

He married a woman who had four sons. Grown-up boys they were, and lazy.

Like the Queen in the story of Conn-eda, this woman was unkind. Little love had she for Shaun, and she made him work hard.

Poor little lad! He was very young when he had to labor like a full grown man, while the sons of his stepmother rested or played.

Shaun was always called Shauneen by his father, who loved him dearly. "Shauneen" means "little Shaun." "Een" is the Irish for "little."

THEY FANCIED AMERICA

"Oh, Shauneen, lad," said the father, one night after his return from sea, "'tis tired you look, and worn. Faith! Can the school work be so hard?"

Shaun did not tell his father that the wicked stepmother had kept him from school that day. He did not tell his father that she had made him walk upon an errand, miles and miles away. He did not say that she had beaten him when he returned.

Shaun was often tempted to tell these things to his good, kind father. But he feared to cause the poor man sorrow.

"Sure, and 'twould be a pity to cause him grief, and he so good," the lad had often thought to himself. "And I can bear it all, for have I not himself to love me?"

Shauneen was a brave boy and felt that to whimper to his father would be weak.

He was a sturdy little lad. His hair

was Irish red and his cheeks were
bright and rosy from the damp, rainy
wind. He was strong and manly.

He hated the red petticoat he was
forced to wear. Often he had thought
of putting on the clothing of a real
boy.

But always in his heart, as in the
hearts of other village boys, there
was the fear of the leprechaun!

And if he were stolen away, what
would his dear father do? His dear
father, who loved him!

It was only because of his father that
Shauneen did not give himself to the
fairies.

He would not have been afraid of
the fairies.

THEY HEARD A STRANGE CRY

He would have liked them to take him away. They could not be so cruel as his stepmother.

Sometimes Shaun's stepmother made him mind her baby. He had to carry it upon his back. Many of the

village boys did this sort of thing, and
so it was not the disgrace that it would
be in a present-day city.

He often went down to the shore.

To-day as he approached the shore,
he met a friend. This friend was a girl,
the daughter of a neighbor. Her name
was Eileen. But Shauneen did not call
her that.

She was his little schoolgirl sweetheart, and he called her Dawn. He
called her Dawn because he told her
that she was the dawn of day to him.

"Some day," he said, "'tis myself,
Shaun O'Day, will marry you. Then
you will be in truth my Dawn O'Day."

To-day they looked out across the
great ocean and dreamed of a new

SHAUN STOOD UP WITH THE BABY ON HIS BACK

world out there. They dreamed of America.

And Shaun said, "When I am tall and strong, I shall take you in a ship to America. Och, we'll be after building a houseen in the New Island!"

The New Island was their Irish name for America.

It was a rainy day, but they did not notice it. Rain is nothing to Irish children. And as they talked together on the shore in the drizzling rain, they heard a strange cry.

Louder grew the cry, and suddenly they saw men and women running toward the shore. They heard the women wailing. They heard the tramp, tramp of men's heavy boots.

Shaun stood up, with the baby on his back. He shaded his eyes and looked.

The girl stood, too. She gave a low cry.

"Och, Shauneen!" she moaned. "'Tis a fishing boat has been wrecked! Och,

HE STARTED TO RUN

the poor wives and children of the men 'twere in it!"

And she moaned and rocked back and forth.

The waters made a roaring sound. The sky was leaden gray. The men were working, pulling in the wreck of the boat.

Shaun gave the baby to Eileen. Then

HE FELL UPON HIS FACE

the boy in his red petticoat started to run.

His feet were bare, but he could skim over those rough rocks like a wild animal. His feet never had known shoes.

His ruddy face had gone white. He reached the group of working men and moaning women. Then he fell upon his face, and a great sob came from his heart.

Among the lost men was his own father!

CHAPTER III

COME AWAY

"Come away, O human child!
To the woods and waters wild,
With a fairy hand in hand."
—W. B. YEATS

The sea had taken away Shaun's only loved one.

Shaun O'Day stood upon the banks of the little lake near his village. He stared out across the blue Irish lake. That morning his stepmother had beaten him.

It was several months since the sea accident had taken his father from him. It was several sad, cruel months to the boy Shaun.

HE STARED OUT ACROSS THE BLUE IRISH LAKE

If it had not been for his little Dawn O'Day, Shaun would have run away. He would have run and run—anywhere to get away from this life of hard work and cruelty.

But he did not want to leave little Dawn O'Day. She pleaded with him to stay. She was afraid of the fairies.

To-day he stood beside the lake, and he had a bundle by his side. It was a bulky bundle. He had worked hard all that morning. He had helped the men burn kelp.

Kelp is seaweed. The people burn it and make iodine from what is left of it. Kelp burning is an important occupation in western Ireland.

Shaun had worked hard. His little rough hands burned. His little sturdy body ached. He was hungry.

He had gone home and, seeing the family at dinner, he had helped himself to potatoes.

His stepmother had cried, "Begob, and did I tell you to serve yourself?

Are you, indeed, the King himself?"
With that, she had beaten him.

Now Shaun stood upon the shore of
that blue Irish lake near his village.
He had taken a suit of clothes belonging to one of his stepbrothers. A suit
of boy's clothes it was.

He would put it on. He would stand
by the lake and call to the leprechauns
to take him away. He would work for
the leprechauns. Yes, willingly would
he work and toil for the fairy folk!

He started to undo the paper in
which he had wrapped the clothing. He
heard a sound and looked up. Eileen
was standing before him. It was his
little Dawn O'Day.

"Shauneen, och, Shauneen!" she

SHE PLEADED WITH HIM TO STAY

cried. "What is it you are about to do? And why do you look that way?"

Shaun did not answer. He took her hand. They sat together on the bank of the lake.

"Faith, speak to me, Shauneen!" cried the girl, the tears starting to her eyes. "Speak and tell me that you are not after calling the lep—"

She stopped suddenly. One should not talk about them. They are easily offended.

Shaun kept looking out across the lake, but he held the hand of his little sweetheart. At last he spoke.

"Sure, I am leaving you, Dawn O'Day," he said.

As she started to cry out, he held up his hand and said, "No; do not cry, for I cannot stay. But do not fear that I shall forget you. The dream we made together shall come true. I'll be coming back to you. For there's not a faireen like you in all the world, at all."

Dawn O'Day began to cry.

She sobbed, "Och, don't be after leaving me! Don't be after going to them. Och, 'tis themselves will be keeping you, and never will Dawn O'Day see you again!"

Shaun laughed and stroked her little hand.

"Troth, do not fret, mavourneen," he said. "Sure, you know well I'll be writing to you, and never will I forget you, my Dawn O'Day."

The little girl knew that it was useless to say more. The boy stood up, and she stood, too. They looked into each other's blue eyes.

And then Eileen ran as fast as she could. She ran away from her little friend and sobbed as she ran. She

HE TOOK HER HAND

thought she should never again see her Shauneen.

The boy quickly changed his clothing. He tied a large rock to the red petticoat and threw it into the lake. He stood there in the garments of a boy.

He held out his arms and cried, "Come, leprechauns! Sure, I'm ready to go with you!"

There was no fear in his heart. Any other boy in that village would have trembled at doing such a thing. But other boys were contented at home.

Other boys had mothers and fathers and good homes. They did not want to be stolen away. Shauneen was not afraid.

He stood and called as he stood. He was straight and strong. He would make a splendid helper for a shoe-maker. Why did the fairy shoemakers not come and take him? He stood there until dusk. Then he grew tired and lay down to sleep. He slept long.

"DO NOT FRET, MAVOURNEEN"

It was early dawn when he awoke.

He stood once more and called out, "I am ready to go. Come, leprechauns, come!"

But not a one came. And the lad was puzzled.

Now Shaun was keen. He was one who thought and planned. He did not intend to go back to his stepmother.

He began to wonder whether the tale of the leprechauns was true. Had anyone ever really seen one? Only old Patch, the village shoemaker, and he was half-witted.

But no one had been with Patch when he had seen the leprechaun. No one ever had seen the fairies; but they all believed. They believed so much that they were in daily dread of them.

They left milk upon window sills and made charms to keep the fairies from doing evil. They dressed their boys in red petticoats.

But Shaun would never again wear a

red petticoat. He would never again return to his stepmother.

Even if the fairies did not steal him, he would never return. He would go somewhere. Perhaps to the "New Island''— America! As he was thinking these thoughts, he found

HE TIED A ROCK TO THE PETTICOAT

himself walking toward the shore. There was a weak light in the sky.

"COME, LEPRECHAUNS!   I'M READY TO GO"

The rugged shore was blue in the haze of dawn.

The boy could see a boat. Men were hauling things and making ready to set off for somewhere. Shaun was quick, and before he knew what he had done he had slid into the boat.

He crouched upon the bottom, under a seat. He made himself as small as a bundle of rags.

He lay very still. He felt the boat leave the shore and he heard the men talking and singing. The water rolled the boat about, and sometimes the spray came in and wet the men.

But Shaun was dry and warm under the seat. He hardly breathed.

CHAPTER IV
THE STRANGE LAND

"Out of the old world
Into the new,
True land or fairyland,
Say, which are you?"

"Shaun O'Day has been stolen by the leprechauns!" That was the whisper that buzzed all about the village the next day.

Little Eileen, with swollen eyes, told her mother how she had left the lad on the bank of the lake. She told how he had planned to put on the clothing of a boy and call the fairies. She wept as she told how brave he had been and how he had promised to write to her.

Her mother smiled sadly and said, "Och, the poor lad will never write! Never will Ireland see himself again! Sure, it's lost he is, and he standing by the banks of that lake in the clothing of a man child! For the fairies do be looking for his likes. Well pleased were they surely to find him!"

She sighed, and so did all the rest of the village folk. They all left milk upon their window sills that night.

They spoke together of the Good People and said, "God bless them!"

For, you see, they wanted to win the good will of the fairies.

Shaun's stepmother was as certain as any of the rest that the boy had been stolen.

She said, "And luck to the Good People! May they work the lazy lad and make a man of him!"

She was not sorry for Shaun. But she was sorry for herself that he was not there to work for her any more.

In a few months nobody spoke of Shaun in the village. He was forgotten. He was forgotten by all but little Eileen. She thought of him each day.

And ofttimes she went to the lake and talked to the blue waters. She asked them where the fairies had taken her Shauneen.

But the wind only blew ripples over the blue waters of the lake. And the trees sighed, and Eileen ran home crying.

She did not tell her mother. She kept her secret in her heart and kept her heart open for Shauneen.

Then one day after many months, a letter came to the town. It was for Eileen. It came from a strange land, and everyone in the village was curious about it.

Some of the old folks in the village did not know English. They spoke only Irish. But the children in the village all knew English, for they studied it in school.

The letter to Eileen was written in English. The little girl ran to the side of the blue lake. She opened the letter with trembling fingers.

This is what she read:

"Dawn O'Day, I have traveled far. The many lands I've seen and the many strange things would open wide your eyes. I am in a fairy city. The lights at night do be shining like the stars. And the noise is like a thousand thunders.

"But the shoemaker is kind. I work hard, but I am paid a handsome sum. And I study at night in a fine school. I am happy but for the sorrow of leaving you. Keep in your heart your faith, for I'll be coming back to get you.

Your Shaun."

When Eileen walked back to the village with her letter clasped in her hand, a crowd of children surrounded her.

"And what is in it?" shouted one

"Are the fairies themselves writing to you?" laughed another.

Eileen shook her curls and would not answer.

One cried, "Och, you cannot keep it secret at all, at all! 'Tis from himself —Shaun O'Day, and 'tis from America!"

The crowd set up a loud roar. "Yes, yes, we know! From America! We saw the mark! 'Tis a fine secret you'd keep, Eileen!"

Eileen's face became red with anger.

"Stop!" she cried. " 'Tis not true! He's with the fairies! He's in a fairy city! 'Tis himself says so!"

But the crowd only laughed the more

loudly. "Ho! A fairy city! And why, then, is the letter marked with the mark of America?"

Eileen had wondered, too, about this. She wondered about the postmark. It said "U. S. A." And that meant United States of America.

" 'Tis a trick of the fairies!" she cried, believing it herself. "A trick to put us off their track! 'Tis himself that's working for the fairy shoemaker in a fairy city!"

She then told them what Shaun had said about the lights at night and the thunder noise. She told how he was receiving pay for his work and about the school to which he went.

They stopped shouting and listened.

Their jaws fell open. They were forced to believe that Shaun was truly in the land of the leprechaun!

Still, some were doubt-ful and went away wag-ging their heads and sneering.

" 'Tis said that in great cities in the New World such things do be," said one.

MARJORIE

But Eileen was happy. No matter where Shaun was, she knew that he was well. She knew that he thought of her and that they would meet again some day.

Letters came often after that. In each one were tales of great wonder. Even the most doubtful of the villagers had to admit that the boy was with the fairies.

He told of strange people, of amusements, of towers touching the sky, and of sights that dazzled his eyes.

Shaun had traveled all the way to a big American city. A bright, strong lad was he.

He could always find ways of working himself along. On ships and trains, in motors, and upon his two feet he traveled.

When he arrived in the strange city across the sea, he sold papers on the streets.

His clear Irish voice rang out with its brogue. Many persons smiled as they listened to the fresh young voice of Shaun O'Day from Connemara.

But one man stopped and spoke to the lad. He, too, was an Irishman. He spoke kindly to Shaun.

The boy told him about his trip and the strangeness he felt in this new land. So this Irishman, Pat O'Leary, took Shaun to his shop.

Pat O'Leary was a shoemaker. He had a tiny shop on a side street in the great city. Here he worked at his trade and lived in a dingy room in the back of the shop.

'Twas thus that Shaun O'Day found a home. And 'twas thus that he started to work for a shoemaker. Pat O'Leary was not a fairy shoemaker. But a good fairy was he to the Irish lad.

He was wrinkled and bent. He might have been an old leprechaun who had lost his way upon earth. He was jolly and smiling, with a joke ever upon his lips.

Shaun lived and worked with Pat and was happy. At night he went to school in the big city and learned many things.

TELLING STORIES OF HIS LAND

The bright lights, flickering on and off, made him blink his eyes. The tall towers and buildings made his neck stiff with looking up.

The noise of the traffic and whistles and motors and people made his ears tingle.

But he loved it and wrote each week to his little friend in Ireland and told her of the magic of it all. He told it with a twinkle in his Irish eyes as he wrote.

He knew she would think he was with the fairies. He knew she, too, would think this big city fairyland if she were here with him.

So he smiled to himself as he wrote to her. And the smiles tumbled down from his lips to the paper on which he wrote.

And when Eileen received the letters those same smiles jumped up and settled on her own two pretty lips. She liked to think that her Shaun was in a fairy city. He knew she would like to think it.

So he went on telling her about the wonders, without ever saying he was in the city of New York.

It was a simple jest. He would not have deceived her for worlds. But that twinkle made him play with her. It made him write letters that read like fairy tales.

And sometimes he wrote verse like this:

> Towers tall
> Make Shauneen small
> Feel like nothing
> At all, at all!

Years went by. One day a very small

girl came into the shoemaker's shop.

Shaun was growing to be a tall boy now. He was tall and manly. But the Irish bloom was still on his face, with the smile of his country.

A very small girl came into the shop with her nurse. While the nurse talked to Pat O'Leary, the little miss came over and sat upon a stool by the side of Shaun O'Day.

He gave her his Irish smile. She gave him a friendly American smile.

She was a pretty, blond baby, with teeth as white as milk and eyes the brown of tree bark.

It was not long before the Irish lad was telling her the stories of his land. She sat spellbound while he talked of

the fairies. He worked upon a shoe
while he talked.

He told her about the leprechaun.
And she
thought
he might be
one, from
the way he
looked as he
worked upon
that shoe.

HE WORKED UPON ONE SHOE WHILE
HE TALKED

Then her
nurse called,
"Come, Mar-
jorie. We
must go!" Marjorie did not want to go.
She stamped her little foot.

"Come, now," begged Nurse, "and

to-morrow we will be coming back."

You see, Nurse was Irish, too, and she loved to talk with Pat O'Leary.

Marjorie could twine Nurse about her little finger and make her do as she wished. Marjorie could make almost everybody do as she wished, for she was sweet and pretty, and she had dimples.

But sometimes she was very stubborn and naughty. Then she did not look so pretty. Her dimple did not seem to be a fairy ripple when she was cross.

Marjorie and Nurse left the shop. All that day, Marjorie thought of the Irish lad's tales.

The next day they came again, and

the next, and the next. Marjorie loved
to go to the shop each day and listen
to the tales of Shaun O'Day.

But one day a frightful thing happened. Marjorie's dimple was looking
more like a smudge of dirt than like a
fairy ripple.

It was evening. Marjorie heard the
water running for her bath.

She stamped her foot at Nurse and
cried, "I won't take a bath!"

When Nurse called to her that the
bath was ready, Marjorie was nowhere
to be found. She had run away from
her home.

Marjorie ran to the shop of Pat
O'Leary, straight to Shaun O'Day.

Shaun was surprised and shocked to

see the little girl alone and at such a late hour. He was just starting off for his school.

Marjorie wanted the lad to tell her tales. But he shook his head.

"Sure, 'tis the wicked child you are, Miss Marjorie," he said. "And 'tis myself will carry you back to your home."

So saying, he picked her up under his arm and took her to her home. Imagine how surprised her parents were when they saw this sight at their door.

There was Shaun, the red-haired Irish lad, standing with their wee daughter tucked under his big arm. She was kicking and squealing like a little pig.

"Begging your pardon, sir," said

Shaun to Marjorie's father, "I've brought you the young lady of the house!"

Marjorie was sent upstairs to bed. I do not know whether her mother spanked her, but I think she did not. Her mother

KICKING AND SQUEALING LIKE A LITTLE PIG

spoiled her the way everyone else did.

Downstairs, Shaun told Marjorie's father how she had come to the shop. Her father asked Shaun to sit down.

He liked the boy. He asked Shaun about his life. Marjorie's father wanted to know about Ireland, too. Shaun talked with his slow brogue. His blue eyes twinkled with the truth there was in them.

Marjorie's father asked Shaun, "Would you not like to change your home? Come and work for me in this house. I will have you taught the work of a butler, if you will come here and stay. You shall tell Marjorie tales every day."

You see, her father was another who wanted to do everything in the world for this little American Princess.

So it came about that Shaun changed his home and his work. He left the shop of Pat O'Leary. And a letter came to Dawn O'Day in Ireland.

It said: "So here I am in the house of a fairy Princess. She did wave her wand, and I was brought to live here by her father. 'Tis a good man he is, too. And I love the baby Princess well and do be pleasing her with tales of old Ireland.

"I'm learning the trade of a butler. I'm after serving themselves out of golden goblets and glass plates the color of Ireland's green. The table shines with bright crystal and silver. The food is beautiful to look upon.

"Then the pay I do get is indeed grand. 'Tis all to be saved for our wedding day, mavourneen."

CHAPTER V

THE FRIGHTENED GIANT

A giant did call at a fairy ball
  With the wee folk he wanted to play,
But as soon as he lifted his clumsy arm
  He frightened the fairies away.

Then back they all came and they played their game,
  And the giant once more tried to play,
But so quick and so light were the fairies bright
  They frightened the giant away.

When Marjorie's nurse went out, it was Shaun who took Marjorie to play in the park. Sometimes they stayed in the big gardens of Marjorie's home, and Shaun told stories.

But occasionally the little girl liked to go where she would meet her friends.

SHAUN TOLD MARJORIE STORIES IN THE GARDEN

On such a day Shaun and Marjorie were playing ball with the children in the park. They were throwing the ball to one another.

Shaun was standing among them like a giant. He was trying to be gentle as he threw the ball. But all at once his strength let go and over the tree tops went the ball.

"O-oh, what a terrible throw!" sneered a small boy.

Shaun ran and brought back the ball. He tried to be more careful. But once he threw it into the duck pond, and at last he lost it altogether. He heard a child snickering as he came back from an unsuccessful search.

Marjorie said, "Let's go home. I'm tired, anyway."

She looked cross, but she did not say a word to Shaun on the way home.

That night Shaun was dressing to help the butler serve dinner. He looked at his big hands.

He looked at his strong arms and sighed, "Och! Shaun O'Day is too big to be the playmate of a fairy princess!"

But he did not worry until later.

Then that evening when he was helping wash dishes, the cook said, "Watch out, boy. You'll break the dishes yet, with your big, clumsy hands."

He tried so hard to be careful. He tried too hard, perhaps, for what cook had warned him of came to pass. He broke a precious cup and saucer.

The other servants said nothing, but smiled behind their hands.

Cook, however, cautioned, "Mind you don't do that again, boy."

Shaun went to his room with a heavy

heart that night. What was the matter? Was he too big, too clumsy?

Would he never learn to be deft and quick like Perkins the butler? Or neat and brisk like the chauffeur Paul?

Oh, well, he could only try. He could be very careful. But anyway, Marjorie still loved his tales.

He could tell stories and amuse the Princess. That was one thing none of the others could do. He fell asleep smiling.

A few days later, Marjorie told him that she was planning a birthday party. She told him about all the amusements they were to have. Many children were to be asked.

They would have ice cream and cake

and chocolate in the garden under the trees. Shaun would serve them.

They would play games, and Shaun would tell them stories. Oh, that was to be the best part of all, Marjorie thought.

Shaun and the little girl planned the party together. Shaun suggested an Irish game, and Marjorie said it would be fun to play it.

So the day arrived. It was a shiny spring day. It was a pretty sight to see the little boys and girls running about and playing together in the green garden.

Marjorie cried out, "Come now! Shaun will show you how to play his game."

"ONCE UPON A TIME IN OLD IRELAND"

And the tall lad stood among the little children. He tried to make them understand what fun it was to play an old Irish game.

It was a game that Shaun had played and that Shaun's father had played and perhaps Shaun's father's father.

But these young Americans did not like it. They said so. They turned their backs and refused to play it.

So Marjorie said, "Then Shaun will tell us a story."

The children gathered around Shaun and he began: "Once upon a time in old Ireland—"

"Will there be any wars in the story?" asked one of the children—a boy, of course.

Shaun twinkled and replied, "Perhaps."

Then he went on. He was telling a fairy tale. The boys began to realize that it was not about wild Indians and wars. They twisted and fidgeted. They dug their heels into the ground, and

one boy pinched another. He squealed
aloud.

"S-sh!" said one girl. "Stop making
that noise!"

But the boys did not want to listen.

One boy stood up and said, "Who
wants to hear about fairies?"

"I don't! I don't!" yelled the others.

Marjorie frowned.

The boys ran away, shouting, "Come
on! Let's play robbers."

Marjorie said, "They would have
liked Shaun's story. They should have
listened. It was awf'lly 'citing! But he
hardly started to tell it."

By this time the group was scat-
tered. Even the little girls were whispering together.

Shaun got up and walked away. He walked to a bench at the other end of the garden and sat down. He was thinking very deeply.

He sat there until he heard his name called. He had to go into the house to help bring out ice cream and cake and chocolate to Marjorie's guests.

As he served little ice cream boats and flowers and animals, his thoughts were far away. The crystal and gold of the plates and goblets did not seem so lovely as before.

Everything on the table swam before Shaun's eyes. Even the children's faces seemed blurred. He heard their talk and laughter in a dream.

He was very unhappy.

"Oh, Shaun, do look what you're doing! ∙ cried a voice in distress.

Shaun looked in horror at what he had done. He had poured hot chocolate over the tablecloth. It was trickling down over a little girl's dress.

Perkins the butler grabbed the chocolate pot out of Shaun's hand.

He muttered, "Clumsy fellow!" and started mopping up.

The little girl began to cry.

Shaun went into the kitchen for a fresh napkin. When he came out to the party again, he heard the children snickering and whispering among themselves. As he approached the table, they stopped. He knew they were making sport of his clumsiness.

He looked at Marjorie. There were tears in her brown eyes, and she was biting her lip. That night Shaun packed his few things and left a letter for Marjorie.

THERE WERE TEARS IN MARJORIE'S BROWN EYES

He told her that he was too clumsy to stay in the home of a princess any longer. He told her that he should never forget her kindness to him.

Then he wrote another letter and put a stamp on it. He walked out of the big house with the letter in one hand and his old Irish carpet bag in the other.

He walked along the bright city streets until he came to a mail box. He kissed the letter and then dropped it into the box.

Dawn O'Day read the letter a few weeks later in Ireland.

This is what it said:

"My Dawn O'Day—

"At last I am leaving the fairy folk. My fingers have grown too clumsy and my arms too big for the dainty likes of the Good People. Those elves, the children of this bright world, do not be wanting Shaun O'Day any more.

"And so, little Eileen, I am coming

back to you and Ireland. And in my pocket is silver and gold to buy us a wedding and a cottage.

"But the cottage will not be in that New Island. 'Twill be in the old Emerald Isle.   Your Shaun."

Shaun sold everything he had but an old suit of clothes. He bought a ticket on a boat going to England and sailed away from New York.

As the big ship left behind her the great American city, the Irish lad saluted and murmured, "Farewell, fairyland. 'Tis too grand you are for the likes of a simple lad like me. But, och, a wonderful, great fairyland you are!"

Slowly the stately harbor disappeared from view.

PART II

CHAPTER VI

JOHN

"Come cuddle close in Daddy's coat
Beside the fire so bright,
And hear about the fairy folk
That wander in the night."
—ROBERT BIRD

It is to-day in Ireland. Shaun O'Day is married to Eileen. He has made her his Dawn O'Day.

They have built a cottage near the banks of that blue Irish lake. They live there with their children.

Shaun and Dawn O'Day have three children. Their youngest is a red-haired baby girl with the eyes and the name of her mother.

Their oldest is a lanky, freckle-faced

lad who wears the cast-off trousers of
his father. No more do tall boys wear
the petticoats of girls. They are not
afraid of the leprechaun when they
reach the age of ten or twelve years.

But their mothers still keep them
dressed as girls when they are small.
And that is why we find John, the second son of Shaun O'Day, in a red petticoat. He looks very much the way
Shaun himself had looked at that age.

John had been christened Shaun.
But they call him John, because it is to-
day in Ireland. Young Shaun was
called John O'Day.

John had the ruddy complexion giv-
en most of these village lads by the
wind and rain. But he was not as

tough and strong as his father had been. He did not have to work. He could come home from school and do as he pleased. Sometimes, of course, he ran errands for his mother or helped her with household chores. But usually he would go to the shores of the lake and think.

Shaun once found his son thus. He went up to John quietly. He put his hand on the lad's shoulder. John jumped and stood erect, his face white.

"Och, why do you jump with such a great fear, my lad?" asked the father.

John sat down again. He was ashamed. He did not speak.

"Tell me, lad: What is it you fear?" asked the father.

HE WOULD GO TO THE SHORES OF THE LAKE

Then John told his father how some boy in the village had started a tale. The lad had told how, many years ago, Shaun had been stolen away by the leprechauns.

John told how it had happened on the

shores of this very lake. He would not believe it and said so.

Still he often lay on his back by the lake and wondered whether it could be true. Now he asked Shaun to tell him.

Shaun stroked his rough chin. The twinkle he had had as a boy was there in his eyes still. He looked at little John beside him.

"Och, Johneen!" he laughed with his musical laugh. "'Tis indeed a true story."

John's eyes grew big. He stared at his father as though Shaun himself might be one of the Good People.

Then he spread out the red petticoat on the ground. He knew that the red petticoat would protect him.

Shaun looked in amusement at the boy's frightened eyes. Then he grew sober.

He said, "You must not fear the Good People, Johneen!"

John wet his dry lips with the tip of his tongue. He came up closer to his father.

"But didn't they make you work for themselves?" he whispered. "And weren't they after stealing you away, and you wearing the clothes of a boy?"

"Yes, yes," agreed Shaun. But he took his little son's hand and stroked it. "And now," he went on, "if you'll listen, I'll tell you the story."

Shaun began, "When I was a lad I was not so fortunate as you, Johneen. I had to work hard. I was beaten and had not enough to eat. So I determined to go with the leprechaun. I put on the clothes of a boy. I stood by the lake. But never a fairy came at all, at all.

"I was tired and slept, and when I awoke 'twas dawn. I ran to the shore in a daze. I jumped into a boat. I was carried away. Through many countries and on many seas I traveled.

"At last I landed in the fairy city. 'Twas there I met the leprechaun himself."

John's hand squeezed the hand of his father. He edged up closer to the big man.

"But do not be thinking that this leprechaun was wicked," continued Shaun. "No, indeed. Kind he was, and good to me. I worked on the mending of shoes and was paid in silver.

"Then did I work for a little princess in the home of her father. Good People they were, too. And the sight of the beauty of that home would surely have dazzled you.

"Among the precious treasures of that house I worked. With the treasured little Princess did I play until at last—"

Here the big man stopped. His voice grew low and soft. He dropped his head.

John asked in a hushed whisper, "Yes —and what happened?"

"Och, well—lad—I came back to old Ireland. Your mother was waiting for me."

Then Shaun arose and placed his hand on John's shoulder.

He continued, "But remember, son, that the Good People will not harm you. Do not be afraid, at all, for well do they love us. And I do believe that they steal the wee boys because they love them so."

Shaun told this tale to the lad John, so he would never again fear the fairies.

And so well did the plan succeed that John began to love the Good People. Over and over, he thought of what Shaun had told him.

He tried to imagine what the baby Princess looked like. He would shut his eyes and try to picture the wonders of that fairy city.

One day he found himself pretending that he was flying over the city. He started and jumped to his feet.

Why had he been doing this? Did he, too, want to go away with the fairies? Of course not. Why should he want to leave his home, his good parents, his brother and sister?

Laughing aloud, he went back to the cottage. He did not visit the lake for several days.

Then one morning, he was walking by himself in the sunshine. The little sparkling beams of sun made him

"THEY'LL NOT BE WANTING GIRLS AT ALL"

think of the lights his father had told him about in the strange city.

Suddenly he found himself on the banks of the lake. He was on the opposite shore. He sat down.

He wondered whether the lepre-

chaun would steal him if he should
wear the clothes of his big brother.
The brightness of the day and the bird
songs made him light of heart. They
gave him courage.

"Sure, I'll try," he exclaimed to the
blue waters of the lake.

What harm to try? Suppose they
took him. It would be fun to visit
fairyland. He could always come
back. His father came back.

In his new enthusiasm, John stood on
the bank and held out his arms crying,
"Come, fairy Good Folk! Take me
away. I do be wanting to see the wonders of your land!"

But the gentle lapping of the lake
was the only answer to his cry. Then

John realized that he was standing in the red petticoat. He smiled.

"They'll not be wanting girls, at all," he reasoned.

Next day, before anyone in the cottage was astir, John slipped out of the door. He was clad in a suit belonging to his older brother. The trousers hung very low, but he tucked them up. He pulled a cap down over his face.

He ran all the way to the opposite shore of the lake. His heart was pounding, and his breath came in gasps.

He threw himself down on the ground to rest. Bird sounds were all about, and a rustling of leaves. The water was lap-lapping as always.

CHAPTER VII

THE GIRL FAIRY

"To the fairyland afar
Where the Little People are."
—ROBERT LOUIS STEVENSON

Marjorie was now grown up. She looked quite different from the tiny golden-haired girl Shaun had known. She was a tall, slender young lady.

Her dimple still became a fairy ripple when she was happy. When she was cross, it still seemed a smudge of dirt.

Marjorie was often cross now. The reason was a strange one. She had too much to make her happy. She had loving parents and a beautiful home. She had many friends who adored her.

111

She was very beautiful, too. Everything lovely belonged to Marjorie. Even wealth was hers.

MARJORIE WAS NOW
GROWN UP

Her father gave her everything she asked for. She had an automobile. She had a beautiful glossy horse to ride.

She went to jolly parties, and all the boys wanted to dance with her. They sent her boxes of chocolate creams and rare flowers.

But Marjorie was not happy with all this. She wanted the one thing that she could not have.

Often she spoke about Shaun O'Day. He had written to her from Ireland when he returned. He had sent her a shamrock and his picture. After that, she had never heard from him again.

She had cried bitterly for many days after Shaun's departure. She had blamed her rude companions for having insulted the Irish lad. She wanted him back.

But of course Shaun never went back to America. He was too happy in Ireland. You know why he was happy. He had his Dawn O'Day and his little children.

So he hardly ever thought of the baby Princess in "fairyland." He was too busy working hard to make a living for his family. He had so little money. But it did not make him unhappy. Sometimes it is a good thing when people have to work. It makes them happy.

You see how discontented Marjorie was. And she had so much! But she finally found a wish that seemed impossible to grant.

When she knew that she might never have Shaun again, she wanted him more than ever. She pleaded with her father to send for him. But that was one thing her father would not do.

He knew that the lad could never be

SHAUN HAD THE DREAMS OF IRELAND

happy in this land. He knew that
Shaun had the dreams of Ireland in his
heart. Shaun belonged in Ireland.

Many years passed, and Marjorie
never forgot Shaun. She often looked
at the young men who danced with her
or who took her to the theater.

She often thought, "He is not so nice
as Shaun O'Day!"

She imagined Shaun even finer than
he was. She had really forgotten what
he was like, and she made a prince of
him in her thoughts.

"I shall never be happy until I find
Shaun O'Day once more!" she said.

One day Marjorie asked her father if
he would take her abroad. She wanted
to visit the countries of Europe. Her

father consented, and the family sailed away on a fine ship.

They were going to France and Germany and Italy and many other countries. They had not thought of going to Ireland. But Marjorie knew that they were going to Ireland!

And in Ireland, poor little John O'Day sat by the lake waiting for the fairies. He had waited there for many days. At first he sat very still with the clumsy trousers rolled up his legs and the big cap falling over his eyes.

He sat still and listened for a sound. He heard only the lake lapping.

Then he began to bring his books along. He liked the books about Ireland that they gave him at school.

—LOOKED AT THOSE PICTURES FOR HOURS AND HOURS

He thought the pictures of Dublin and Belfast looked very like that fairy city of which his father had told. He looked at those pictures for hours and hours. And he waited there by the banks.

He always changed to his red petticoat before he went home. He did not want anyone to know what he was doing. Some might laugh at him.

His mother would be frightened and hold him close. She might make him promise never to do it again. Then he would never see the fairies.

His brother could not imagine what had become of his old suit of clothes. He had to wear his Sunday suit until he could make enough money to buy a new suit. But the days slipped by, and the boy waited in vain for the leprechaun. The longing for adventure was great in his heart.

One day he stepped to the edge of the lake and cried out in a loud voice, "Arrah, 'tis long I've waited and tired

I am! Come, Good Folk, come! Give to the son of Shaun O'Day the great wonders of your fairy powers!"

As his voice died down, he stepped back from the edge of the water. He looked about cautiously. Then his heart gave a leap. He had heard a tiny sound. It was not the lapping lake. It was not the wind in the trees.

It was surely a fairy. And as he was thinking these thoughts, he saw her.

She came gliding over the ground like a rainbow. Her gown was lavender and blue, flowing and billowy. Her dainty little shoes were snow-white. And her hair was spun gold.

A many-colored scarf twined about her neck and fluttered in the breeze.

HE STARED OUT AT THE LOVELY VISION

There was a beautiful perfume in the air as she appeared.

The boy backed into the bushes. He stared out at the lovely vision. His eyes were wild with fear.

The beautiful creature came closer.

She held out her hand and smiled. Her hand was snow-white. Her smile was a sunbeam, with a dimple in it.

"Do not be afraid," said her clear, sweet voice. "You called the fairies, son of Shaun O'Day?"

John nodded, but could not speak. His mouth was dry.

"I have come at your command," she smiled. Then she led John out and looked at him for a long time. She was smiling kindly. At last she spoke.

"You are the son of Shaun O'Day. And I am the fairy Princess who once stole Shaun from the leprechaun. I used to hear his fine stories of Ireland. I loved to listen to him. He used to play with me in fairyland. Did he tell you?"

John looked into her sparkling brown eyes and said, "Sure, and he did. He told me about it all. And I did be wanting to go with the fairies, too."

She laughed a silvery laugh and put her arm about John. "And so you shall," she said. "Come with me. Let me show you to our fairy chariot."

She led him away. They walked for quite a while until they came to a dusty road. It was a road on which many donkey carts travel, but few automobiles.

She drew him to the side of a shining automobile. It was the most beautiful thing John had ever seen.

"Enter, Shaun," said the girl fairy.

John looked at her for just an instant

"YOU ARE THE SON OF SHAUN O'DAY"

with a question on his lips. She had called him Shaun. Why?

But she stopped his question and said, "We shall fly over the ground now. Hold on tight."

For the next hour, the boy John

hardly breathed with excitement. He was being carried over the ground faster than ever he had gone in his life.

Trees and fields and pigs and donkeys flew by. Thatched cottages seemed to dart out at them and then disappear.

The girl fairy sat at the big wheel of the car and only smiled at him occasionally. She said never a word.

At last they drew up at the side of a lonely road. She stopped the flying car. She turned to him.

She said, "Now Shauneen, what do you want me to do for you?"

John took a deep breath and clutched the side of the car.

Then he answered slowly, "Faith!

I'm after longing to visit fairyland."

The girl fairy's smile vanished for a moment. Then she took his hand in hers and spoke seriously.

"Shauneen," she said, "I cannot take you there. But I can show you a land as beautiful as fairyland. I can take you all about your own land, Ireland. Do you know that the poets have called Ireland fairyland? Do you know that there is no greener spot on earth?"

John's eyes glowed.

He answered, "Indeed, I do know it. And I'm forever seeing the pictures in the school books. Sure, I do believe I'd rather be seeing Ireland than any fairyland at all!"

"ENTER, SHAUN," SAID THE GIRL FAIRY

"Good!" laughed the girl fairy. Then she grew serious again as she said, "But Shauneen, you must promise your fairy that you will not speak of this to anyone at all. You must also ask your father to come to the shore of the lake to-morrow morning while you

are at school. Tell him that there is
some one who would speak with him on
a serious matter. But do not say any
more. If you obey these two com-
mands, your fairy will come again. She
will come for you on the shores of the
lake. She will take you to all parts of
your own beautiful country."

John promised to carry out her
wishes. Again they flew over the
ground until at last they were back at
the spot whence they had started.

Then John stepped out of the glistening automobile. The girl fairy
threw him a kiss and was off in a cloud
of dust.

CHAPTER VIII
OVER THE GREEN LAND

Above is so blue
And below is so green;
We are sailing away
In our flying machine.

John was in school. But his mind was not on his lessons. For the first time, the letters in his book swam before his eyes. The teacher's voice seemed far away.

He was thinking of the girl fairy and of his coming trip with her. She had told him to say nothing, and he must obey her. But he could not help thinking about her. Surely she was good and would let no harm befall him.

His father had told him that the Good People were kind and loved little boys. So he smiled and paid no attention to his school work.

The teacher set him in a corner with a dunce's cap on his head.

In the meantime, John's father was walking to the shore of the lake. He wondered who wanted to see him. John had told him that it was an important matter.

He scratched his red head and puzzled. He waited on the banks of the lake until he heard a light step behind him.

He turned and saw John's girl fairy. She walked over to him silently. He jumped up and looked at her. Shaun

O'CONNELL STREET AND NELSON'S COLUMN, DUBLIN

thought he had never seen so exquisite a being. She spoke.

"You are Shaun O'Day," she said softly. She held out something and continued, "Please take this."

Shaun took from her graceful white hand a slip of paper. She kept looking into his eyes.

"Read it, Shaun," she said.

Shaun opened the paper. His eyes fell on his own boyish handwriting and a shamrock pasted across the top of the letter.

"Faith, 'tis a letter I wrote, myself, when I was a lad!" he exclaimed.

The girl fairy only smiled and kept looking into Shaun's eyes.

"Begob!" he suddenly shouted, looking hard at the girl fairy. "'Tis Miss Marjorie, the baby Princess!"

"Yes, Shaun," answered Marjorie happily. "'Tis Marjorie come all the way from fairyland to see you."

Then the two sat down on the bank. Shaun took off his coat and spread it on the ground for the girl to sit upon. They talked and laughed and remembered old times together.

Suddenly Marjorie grew serious and said, "Shaun, I have seen your son!"

Shaun looked surprised.

Marjorie continued, "Shaun, I want you to help me. I want to give a great pleasure to your little John."

Then she told Shaun how John had seen her the previous day. She told

DUBLIN IS QUAINT AND ANCIENT

how John had believed her to be a fairy. She told Shaun that she had promised to take the little lad on a trip through Ireland.

She finished by saying, "I want to make him happy, Shaun, as you made me, long ago. Will you say that I may take him?"

Shaun's eyes were moist. He felt very grateful to the girl.

He replied in a low voice, "Och, Miss Marjorie, you are indeed no fairy, but a great good angel!"

Marjorie jumped up gayly and cried, "Then you will let him go with me, Shaun?"

"And sure you know well I will, Miss Marjorie. 'Tis a great good you will be doing for my lad. It is surely," he said.

Marjorie looked very serious then. And she bowed her head.

Her words were whispers as she said, "If it is a great good, then it is the first great good I have ever done. I have

A JAUNTING CAR

been very selfish, Shaun. Everyone has always done for me. This is the first time I have ever done something to give some one else pleasure. And, oh," she suddenly clasped her hands together and smiled radiantly, "it is a wonderful feeling! It has made me happy, Shaun."

She kissed his rough brown hand and turned on her dainty heel. She fled before Shaun could utter a sound.

"Well, begob, begorra!" he at last sputtered, scratching his head and wrinkling his nose. "Now isn't it a great wonder?"

Then, as if some breeze had contradicted him, he nodded his head and said loudly, "It is surely!"

It was several days before Marjorie's next visit to the lake.

Although the little boy John went thither daily and waited longingly, no girl fairy appeared. But he never doubted that she would come. He knew she would keep her promise. And she did.

At last, one day, she came tripping over the ground, laughing and calling, "Shauneen, Shauneen, 'tis I!"

John trembled. But he smiled at her and held out his hand.

To-day she was not dressed in fluttering, light-colored garments. Instead, she had on a brown leather coat. She wore a little round cap.

She carried a small coat, which she held out to John.

"Put this on quickly and come, for our air chariot awaits us," she exclaimed, helping John put on the fine warm coat.

Again they walked to the shining

LOVELY LAKES IN PHOENIX PARK, DUBLIN

white automobile, and then they drove and drove. At last they came to a large field. It was an air port, a place where airplanes land.

The girl stopped her car. John saw a winged machine standing in the center of the field. It was a strange, terrible thing to the boy John.

"Come," said Marjorie, taking him by the hand. "It is our airplane. We shall fly over the green land together!"

An airplane! John had seen airplanes before, but never like this. He had seen them circling far up in the sky.

He could often hear the whirring sound they made. They usually were so high that they looked to the lad like small birds.

But this one was a monster. There was a pilot ready to start the plane and carry them off. They stepped inside the monster. John sat beside Marjorie, and she held his hand. He edged up close to her.

The plane's motor started. They began to rise from the ground. Oh,
it was like be-
ing a bird, John
thought. It was
even like being a
fairy.

He stole a
glance at the girl
fairy. She was
beaming at him.

"Do you like
this, Shauneen?"
she asked.

SHE GAVE JOHN A HAND-
SOME LITTLE TRAVEL-
ING BAG

"Faith, 'tis sure-
ly a great wonder! And you the good
angel!" breathed the boy.

Marjorie remembered Shaun had

said those same words to her. She felt happier than she had felt ever before in her life.

It was a trip that John O'Day never would forget. John would remember that trip to his ninetieth birthday.

They flew in the plane to the city of Dublin. They stopped at a fine hotel, and the girl fairy gave John a handsome little traveling bag with everything in it that he needed.

There were soft, fine pajamas. There was a new suit of clothes. There was a cap to match his coat, with fine socks and shoes.

They started out early the next morning to see all of Dublin town. A great city it seemed to John, with its

SUGARLOAF MOUNTAIN NEAR DUBLIN

SOME OF THE SIGNS WERE WRITTEN IN IRISH

strange noises and its jostling mobs on the streets.

In the center of O'Connell Street stands Nelson's Pillar. It is a thin, tall pillar. Inside there are one hundred and sixty-six steps which wind right up to the top. John and Marjorie walked up to the top and stood looking down on the streets below.

John noticed later when they walked in the streets that some of the signs were written in Irish.

John was just learning to read Irish in school. So he could read some of the signs.

School children have to study the Irish language in that part of Ireland called the Free State. The Free State is free from Great Britain and has its own government. It is the southern part of the country, and Dublin is the capital.

The northern part of Ireland is still under the government of England.

A SCHOOL WHERE THEY TEACH THE IRISH LANGUAGE

The County Galway, wherein John's village stood, belongs to the Free State.

Policemen on the streets of Dublin wear caps with silver harps on their visors. You know that the harp is the symbol of Ireland, and it is used on the new flag of the Irish Free State.

Dublin is a quaint and ancient city. There are few automobiles on the streets.

One sees many jaunting cars, which are funny little high carts with a seat on each side and big wheels. People sit with their legs hanging over the sides, while the driver sits up on the high box and drives an old thin horse.

There are also many bicycles whirling along in Dublin.

Children seem to be everywhere. Some look very poor, indeed. Some beg the wealthy people for money. There are many beggars. They crouch beside buildings and on the steps of

ST. PATRICK'S COLLEGE, DUBLIN

churches. John and his fair guide visited Phoenix Park in Dublin. After Yellowstone Park in the United States, Phoenix Park is the largest in the world.

It is very beautiful, too. It has a fine

PHOENIX PARK, DUBLIN

zoo, and lovely lakes, walks, and drives.

The Royal Hibernian Military School in Phoenix Park is used by the Free State Irish Speaking Union as a school to teach the Irish language to young men.

THE COUNTRY OF TOM MOORE

They visited St. Patrick's College where a large number of students attend. This is a fine old college.

They left Dublin after seeing everything of interest there. They left in a drizzling rain in Marjorie's big white

motor car. It had been brought to them
from the flying field to Dublin. It
seemed to John that things were always being brought to Marjorie in a
magical way. And why not? Marjorie
was a fairy! Now they motored to the
Vale of Avoca.

This is the beautiful woodland spot
where Tom Moore, the Irish poet,
wrote much of his poetry.

His famous words are:

"There is not in this wide world a valley so sweet
As the vale in whose bosom the bright waters meet."

CHAPTER IX

WANDERING

"Over hill, over dale,
Through bush, through brier,
Over park, over pale,
Though flood, through fire,
I do wander everywhere."
—WILLIAM SHAKESPEARE

While John traveled with his good fairy, his mother and father sat before their fireside. They talked for hours about the lad's good fortune.

Of course Shaun explained to his wife that the girl was no fairy. He told Dawn O'Day that she was Marjorie, the baby Princess, for whom he had worked so long ago.

Dawn O'Day was pleased to think

how much her boy was learning. She loved to think that some day little John might be a great, wise man.

And the boy was indeed learning, and seeing all manner of wonders. Together he and Marjorie visited the Giant's Causeway, which is in the northern part of Ireland. The Giant's Causeway is a very remarkable place.

It is supposed to have been made by the giants of old. It is believed by some that the queer rocks were built by giants. These great monsters were trying to make a great bridge across the water to join Ireland and Scotland.

Of course this is only a fairy tale. But those huge, queer rocky forms do look as though giants had built them.

The water roars up to the shore and often splashes over those strange, tall rocks. They are probably the result of a terrible eruption by some volcano, or fire mountain, years ago.

The rocks form many peculiar shapes. There is the Giant's Organ— a group of immense rocks resembling a mighty organ.

There is the Wishing Chair, a single column backed by higher ones. It forms a very comfortable chair. And they tell you that if you make a wish there, it will come true. But never must you speak that wish aloud.

There is a well of clear, fresh water within a few feet of the Atlantic Ocean.

THE WISHING CHAIR

There is the gate which stands as the gate to Giant Land.

There are the Giant's Eyeglass, the Chimney Tops, the Loom, and other forms of great size made of these strange rocks. It is no wonder that the people think of giants, when looking at them.

The little boy and his guide visited the mountain of Crough Patrick, one of the sacred places of Ireland.

It is where St. Patrick stood when he banished all snakes and other reptiles from Ireland. This is supposed to have happened in the year 450 A. D.

St. Patrick imprisoned all creeping things in a deep canyon and kept them there. When he was ready to destroy them, he stood upon the summit of the mountain with a bell in his hand.

He stood there and rang that bell. And each time he rang that bell thousands of snakes and other creeping creatures went tumbling into the sea.

In Ireland to-day there are no snakes, toads, or poisonous reptiles. The people believe that it is because St. Patrick destroyed them all, many years ago.

In July many pilgrims climb to this mountain. They pray there to St. Patrick.

John and Marjorie went to the Lakes of Killarney. These are perhaps the best known lakes in all the world. Songs and poems have been written about their beauty.

There are three lakes. Each one has a peculiar beauty of its own. The lakes lie between mountains like brilliant diamonds glistening in an emerald setting.

They tell a legend in Killarney. They say that once no lakes were there at

THE GATE TO GIANT LAND

all. One man living there had a magic well. If he always kept the well covered, no harm would come.

But one night somebody came to the well for water and forgot to cover it. The next morning a great flood had swallowed up the land. The town was completely under water.

Sometimes, the natives say, one can still see, at the bottom of the lakes, this old town with the same old well. The Irish do love to be telling tales of magic.

Blarney Castle is noted for the famous Blarney Stone. It is said that those who kiss the Blarney Stone forever afterward possess the art of flattery and beautiful speech.

You have often heard people say, "You must have kissed the Blarney Stone!"

People who make many compliments are sometimes accused of kissing the Blarney Stone.

Nor is it an easy object to kiss! John
O'Day and Marjorie climbed to the top
of Blarney Castle. There the old stone
hangs from the top of the battlements.
It lies in a peculiar position.

John lay flat and thrust his head
down about three feet through an
opening. He then twisted his neck in
order to kiss the precious stone. A
guard held his feet.

It was a wise thing to do, for it is
over a hundred feet to the ground below! It would be a terrible fall!

As they traveled, they passed beautiful green country. They saw many
pigs and many donkey carts.

In every village they found a war
memorial. Some of these memorials

THE GIANT'S EYEGLASS

stand in the center of the town. Some are very large and beautiful. Others are small. But all mean the same thing. Ireland lost many soldiers in the Great War.

They found few fruits growing in Ireland. Gooseberries are plentiful, and they ate many.

Marjorie found the Irish peasants friendly and kind. Several times they stopped for the night in farmhouses.

The people told Marjorie many wonderful tales as she sat before their firesides. They were very much surprised to find the girl traveling about alone with a young child.

But she only laughed in her easy way, as the old women said, "God be praised, but American girls do be knowing no fear!"

Marjorie always made John go to bed right after dinner. The little boy was tired from his long day's travels. He was tired, too, with seeing and hearing so many new things. So he did not hear the people talking at night. He still

believed his girl fairy was one of the
Good People.

One day they were stopping in a
small village. Marjorie left John alone
with the car and went into a shop to
buy some cakes.

A group of little boys came over to
the car. Their eyes were very curious,
indeed.

They began to talk to John. When
they heard his accent they knew at
once that he was Irish.

One boy said, " 'Tis surely a rich
American lady driving the automobile?"

John looked at him in a pitying manner. "And don't you know a fairy when
you see one?" he asked.

BLARNEY CASTLE

The boys' mouths opened. They stared at John.

Then one boy came close to John and cried out, "Arrah, 'tis no fairy, at all, at all! 'Tis an American lady from across the seas!"

John faced the boy. There was a frown on his face.

"You'll not be standing there saying that again!" he said. "'Tis herself is one of the Good People!"

The boy laughed again. "Och, you know well she is no fairy!"

"She is!" yelled John.

"She is not!" shrieked the boy.

John rolled up his sleeves. He hit the boy.

When Marjorie came out of the shop

she found her young friend in a fierce battle. She separated the boys and thrust John into the car. He was waving his arms and shouting.

Marjorie jumped into the driver's seat. She started the car, and off they went.

John's clothing was torn. He was bruised. The boy with whom he had fought was larger than he. But John knew that he had left the other boy as bruised and torn as he was himself. So he smiled.

Marjorie drove for a while in silence. Then she asked, "John, why did you fight?"

John told her the reason. She bit her lip and was silent again.

SHE SEPARATED THE BOYS

Then she said, "John, how do you know that I am a fairy?"

The little boy answered promptly, "Because I was after calling the fairies that day by the lake. And because I did take off my petticoat and put on the clothes of a boy."

"Do you believe that was the reason I took you away?" asked Marjorie.

"I do," answered John firmly. "And," he continued, "if I had been in the petticoats of a girl, you would never have noticed me at all."

"Why?" Marjorie queried.

"Sure, and the Good People do be wanting the boys to work for themselves. They'll not be noticing girls, and they so weak!" John answered.

THEY PASSED DONKEY CARTS

Marjorie frowned. Then she said, "But I have not made you work."

John looked at her quickly and replied, "Och, no! But 'tis willing I am to work for you now. Only—" He hesitated.

"Only what, John?" asked the girl.

"I'll not be wanting to stay away forever from my mother and father," was the reply.

Marjorie put an arm about his shoulder.

"Do you know that we are almost at your home now?" She laughed gayly. "Look about you!"

The little boy was amazed to see that they really had returned. They were on the same dusty road whence they had started their trip so many days ago.

Marjorie drew the car up to the side of the road and stopped it.

"Now you may jump out and run home to your mother and father," she said.

A WAR MEMORIAL IN EVERY VILLAGE

John O'Day just stood and stared at her.

"And you'll not be asking me to work at all?" he questioned, with wondering eyes.

Marjorie shook her head and smiled.

"Och," cried the boy, "but I want to do something for you!"

Marjorie stroked his hand and replied softly, "It is not necessary, Shauneen. Your father did so very much for me many years ago. I am glad that I can now give his son a little happiness."

"And will you not be coming back again to the lake, good fairy?" asked John.

Marjorie's smile faded as she answered, "Shauneen, I am not a fairy. You must believe that. I shall come back to the lake to see you. But I shall come to bid you good-bye, for I am going back to America."

For a moment John was almost go-

THEN HE KISSED HER HAND

ing to believe her. His throat felt
choky. Then suddenly he shook his
head and laughed aloud.

"Sure, 'tis not so at all, at all!" he
laughed. "There's not a girl in all the
world as beautiful as you. There's not
a girl in all the world so good and kind,

Faireen. Och, no! Not even the girls from the land of America! 'Tis indeed the fairy you are!"

The little boy climbed out of the car. He saw a shamrock growing by the side of the road. He ran and picked it. He gave it to Marjorie. Then he kissed her hand and ran as fast as he could.

He left the girl staring after him in real amazement. So he would not believe her! He thought that she was a fairy! Ah, well, she must certainly show him in some way that what she told him was true.

She did not want to leave Ireland and feel that she had deceived the boy. Still, she loved to think that he believed her to be a fairy.

It was a beautiful dream to John.
She did not like to disturb that beautiful dream. Puzzled, she shook her
head as she started her car. Then she
was off, down the dusty road.

CHAPTER X

BECAUSE HE IS IRISH

"I cannot see fairies.
I dream them.
There is no fairy can hide from me.
I keep on dreaming till I find them."
—HILDA CONKLIN

John O'Day walked slowly through the village. He walked through the village because he wanted all the boys to see his fine suit.

The fine suit was a bit torn and soiled from the fight he had had. Still John was proud of it.

He went home by way of the village. He did not go by way of the lake. As he walked down the village street, the people stared at him.

176

"And where are you going, John O'Day?" called one boy.

"Sure, I'm not going," answered the little lad. "I'm after coming back from where I was!"

He marched along. They all stood with staring eyes and watched him.

He came to the cottage of his parents, and when they saw him they were delighted.

Of course, John told his mother and father everything.

He tried to tell it all before he went to bed. But the evening was too short and his tale too long. He was fairly bursting with the great trip he had had.

He even had a tale of wonder for his

wee sister. He held her on his knee
while he told about the big zoo in Dublin.

"Sure, and there's every kind of animal there," he went on, his eyes flash-
ing. "Sure, I was after seeing a terrible, big creature. 'Twas an elephant
they called it. And 'tis a square animal
with a tail in front of it and a tail behind it!"

"Glory be!" cried his mother.

Shaun smiled behind his pipe. The
baby gurgled.

The older brother pretended that he
was not very much interested. He was,
though. He was greatly excited with
John's tales.

Then his father said, "But, Johneen,

you do not really believe that your guide was a fairy?"

"Sure, and the best one in all fairyland," answered John stoutly.

Shaun scratched his head thoughtfully.

"Och, Johneen," he said, "you do not believe that surely."

But John answered, "I do!"

Shaun then drew the boy over to his chair. He took John on his lap.

"Listen, son," he said.

He told the child the same thing that Marjorie had told him. He told John that Marjorie was really a girl from America.

But John replied as he had replied to Marjorie in the car. He said that there

could not be a girl so lovely and kind as
she. He insisted that Marjorie could
only be a fairy!

Several days went by. John told everyone in the village about his trip. He
talked of nothing else. He had gone to
the lake day after day, but the girl
fairy had never appeared.

He did not give up hope, however.
He felt she would keep her promise
and come again to see him.

Then one day little John received a
package and a letter. In the package
were several beautiful books.   He
asked his father to read the letter to
him.

Shaun read:

"Dear Shauneen: To-morrow I am

coming to the lake to say good-bye to you. Please be there. Marjorie."

Shaun folded the letter and gave it back to his son.

Then he said, "You see, she is an American girl. Her father and mother are going to take her back to America. They brought her over, and they also bought her that car. They arranged for her to take you on that fine trip. Don't you see now that she surely is not a fairy?"

But John did not answer. He shook his head stubbornly. Suddenly Shaun had an idea.

He said, "I must show you then." He put his two hands on the boy's shoulders and looked into his eyes. "To-morrow," he said, "when you go to meet her at the lake you must wear the red petticoat!"

John looked frightened.

He cried, "Och, father, she'll not be talking to me at all—and I in girl's clothes!"

Shaun said, "Sure, that is just what she will do. She'll know you well. She'll talk to you. Then you will believe at last that she is no fairy!"

The morning came. John dressed as usual in his red petticoat. He took the books that Marjorie had sent him and ran to the lake. He was there with the first birds. He was there with the sleepy sun.

The sleepy sun was just waking up.

But John O'Day had been awake for many hours. He had been so very much awake with his thoughts.

He thought and thought about Marjorie. He wondered and wondered whether Marjorie would recognize him. If she should speak to him, he would know that she really was a girl. He would know that she was not a fairy.

If she passed him by, he would be sure that she was a real fairy. Oh, he felt so sure that she was a fairy!

But at the same time he wondered just a little bit why she tried to make him believe she was not. Was it because the Good People do not want folks to be talking about them?

SHE WAS SMILING DOWN AT HIM

Maybe it was that. They like to give happiness to people. But they do not want people knowing that it is they giving the happiness.

They do not ask thanks. They do not

look for praise. The Good People are modest.

But soon John would know about his lovely friend. She would soon appear and look for him. If she passed him by, his heart would beat with joy. He would know then.

And he would call out to her, "It is I! It is your Shauneen! Do you not know me?"

Then she would stop and he would laugh at her and jolly her.

He would say, "You could not be fooling me, good fairy. Isn't it myself knows a fairy when I see one?"

He chuckled to himself. She should not be fooling John O'Day!

He opened one of the lovely books

which Marjorie had sent him. He began to look at it. It was a beautiful book with colored pictures in it. It had grand pictures of cities in it.

There were pictures of Irish cities and French cities and American cities.

John grew so interested in looking at the pictures that he did not hear a step behind him. He did not see Marjorie standing behind him. She was smiling down at him as he sat all wrapped in joy and delight.

He was remembering his trip through the cities whose pictures he now looked at in a book. He was in Dublin again. He had jumped right into the book and was believing that he could hear the dull sounds of the city. He was believing that he could see the many people and cars and curious sights.

Marjorie watched him for a few moments. She knew John O'Day, though he wore a girl's petticoat. She had come to bid him good-bye, for she was leaving for her own country.

But she could not disturb him as he sat there. She could not disturb John O'Day

IT WAS THE PICTURE OF HIS GIRL FAIRY

while at his books. Nor could she disturb his dreams.

She knew well that if she spoke to him now, he would know that she was not a fairy. He had told her that "fairies do not be speaking to girls," and Marjorie could not disturb the little boy's beautiful dream of her.

So she scribbled a note and left it on a flat rock. The note told John that she had come and gone. It said that Marjorie was sorry she had not seen her Shauneen again. But she left him with his dream of her.

When John lifted his head and heart out of the pages of that grand book, he stood up and looked about. He saw the letter and opened it.

Of course he could not read it, but he found something else with the letter which he kissed. It was the picture of his girl fairy. She had left it there.

And now John O'Day knew that she had come and gone.

Thought he, "She did not know the little figure in the red petticoat was her friend Shauneen! No; she did not notice this little girl at all, at all. Fairies do not be speaking to little girls."

She had gone. But she had left behind her the picture of a girl fairy. She had left that picture on a flat rock.

And she had left it, too, in the Irish heart of John O'Day, who had the dreams of his country.

Marjorie will always remember the

HE WILL ALWAYS KEEP HIS DREAMS

little boy. She will go back to America and always remember the boy who called her a good fairy. She will try really to be a good fairy because of that.

She will not think so much about herself any more. But she will try to give pleasure to others because of the pleasure she finds in doing it.

And as John O'Day grows older, perhaps he will find out the truth about Marjorie. But he will always be wanting to believe that she was a girl fairy, even if he finds that she was not.

He will always want to keep his dreams, because he is Irish.